If Not Me, then What Could It Be?

Bernadette Holmes

Illustrated by Abbey Bryant

"If Not Me, then What Could It Be?

First paperback edition November 2022

Illustrated by Abbey Bryant

ISBN 978-0-578-37307-2

To my kiddo,

Your existence has been a gift that I will forever cherish; for it is because of you that I am here today. I gave you life and you saved mine. Together, we will save many.

Love,
Mommy

Josiah can barely contain her excitement. She smiles and squirms in her seat, thinking about all the plans she and her mom have for the weekend.

"Mommy promised we would build a fort of pillows and watch a movie tonight! Tomorrow we are going to the fair and I'm going to get the biggest cotton candy they have! Then, we are going to my favorite restaurant for dinner!"

Josiah skips all the way home from the bus stop and burst
through the door with a twinkle in her eyes, yelling,
"Mommy, mommy, I'm home!
Are you ready to go?"

She drops her book bag at the door, kicks off her shoes, and
tosses her jacket across the room.

When her mother doesn't answer, she begins to look for her, going room to room.

Josiah looks in the kitchen.

She looks in the bathroom. "Mommy", Josiah says, starting to get worried.

She gets to her mother's bedroom and the door is shut.

She knocks a few times. "Come in, kiddo", her mom says, speaking above a whisper. Josiah opens the door to find her mom still in bed.

"Mommy, why are you still in bed, are you ok?" Her mom lets out a long, slow sigh.

"Hey there Jo Jo Bear." Josiah leans in and gives her mom a big hug. "I'm okay, just not having a very good day."

Josiah notices the tears in her mother's eyes and knows what is coming next.

"No movie night or building the fort of pillows?", she asks with her head down. "Can I take a raincheck?", her mother says? "How about tomorrow?"

Josiah is devastated, as she walks to her room, "Why does this always happen to me?"

"Why can't my mommy ever do the things she says she's going to do?"

Josiah climbs off the bed slowly, "sure",
as she closes the door behind her.

Josiah peels her eyes open, glancing at her calendar and notices the Ferris Wheel marked for today.

She jumps up and heads to the kitchen!

"Good morning Josiah, are you ready for today?" "Oh yeah! I can't wait to get on all the rides and have pink cotton candy!"

Her mother laughs, "Well let's start with breakfast. How about you set the table while I finish up the pancakes."

While setting the table, she can't help but to think that today will be different. "Mommy will be in a great mood because who could be sad at the fair, right?"

As they turn into the fairgrounds, Josiah is
beaming from ear to ear. Her mother gives her a
big smile, as her eyes fill with water. "Mommy,
are you crying because you're so excited?"

Her mother laughs as she wipes her eyes,
"I guess so Jo Jo bear."

"Mommy, I had the best time ever! Did you have a good time?"
"Of course, kiddo. I always have the best time when we are together."

"But, I thought we were going to have dinner at my favorite restaurant?" Her mother replies, "Oh, Josiah, I think we've had enough fun for today. I am exhausted. How about we just order pizza instead?"

As the tears stream down her face, Josiah asks,
"Why are you always so sad, Mommy?
Why do you always want to sleep?"

Am I making you cry because I
don't pick up my toys?
Are you mad at me?"

Her mother hugs her tight, "Oh Jo Jo Bear, I wish
you could understand. Maybe when you're older.
I could never be sad because of you;
I love you more than anything."

Even though Josiah had a wonderful day at the fair, she can't help but to wonder about what her mother said. "Why does Mommy think I won't understand? Why do I have to wait until I'm older? If she's not sad because of me, then what could it be?"

Josiah sheds a tear, as she fastens the last button on her favorite pajamas. "Jo Jo, the pizza is here", her mother yells from the living room.

Josiah joins her mother on the couch and stares at her pizza. Pepperoni with pineapples is usually her favorite, but today, it just doesn't taste the same.

"This pizza isn't the only thing different around here", Josiah says to herself. She takes a few more bites and tries to remember the good times with her mother.

Memories of her playing and laughing bring a smile to Josiah's face. "That's it! I will make a happy list so she can smile again!" "Mrs. Goodjoy, the school counselor, said this list can help when we are feeling sad and blue and can't figure out what to do."

Josiah takes off to her room and does a canon-ball into the middle of the bed. With her notepad and pen in hand, she eagerly gets started.

Just as she is collecting the last item on her list, her mother calls for her. "Coming, Mommy."

Carrying the basket, she makes her way down the hall and stops suddenly. She can't believe her eyes.

"The pillow fort!" She climbs in to see her mother waiting for her. "Let's talk kiddo."

"I want you to know that when Mommy is sad, it is never your fault. Sometimes mommies and daddies have sad days, where they may cry and want to sleep more than normal.

Sometimes it's hard to do chores, go to work, and even play with you!"

"But why", says Josiah. "Well kiddo, for some people like Mommy, my brain and my body don't always agree.

One wants to get up and build forts with you, but the other makes me feel like I can't."

"Oh, I understand", says Josiah. "So,
it's not because my room is a mess?"
Her mother smiles,
"No, Jo Jo Bear. I don't
like for your room to be messy,
but it doesn't make me sad."

Josiah then shows her mother the basket. "Mrs. Goodjoy, my school counselor, said that a happy list can help when you are feeling sad and blue, so I made one just for you!" Her mother smiles, "Thank you, kiddo!"

"I just want you to be happy again, Mommy." "I will. Some days, I must work harder at that, but I'm always trying", says her mother.

She quickly slips on the fuzzy socks and gives the teddy bear a squeeze. As they begin to color together, Josiah thinks to herself, "Out of all the things it could be, I understand it's not because of ME."